I'M NOT SCARY...

I'M JUST A DINOSAUR!

words&pictures

© 2025 Quarto Publishing Group USA Inc.
Text © Ben Lerwill 2025
Illustrations © Erica Salcedo 2025

Ben Lerwill has asserted his right to be identified as the author of this work.
Erica Salcedo has asserted her right to be identified as the illustrator of this work.

First published in 2025 by words & pictures,
an imprint of The Quarto Group.
100 Cummings Center, Suite 265D
Beverly, MA 01915, USA.
T (978) 282-9590 F (978) 283-2742
www.quarto.com

EEA Representation, WTS Tax d.o.o., Žanova ulica 3, 4000 Kranj, Slovenia

Assistant Editor: Jackie Lui
Senior Commissioning Editor: Catharine Robertson
Designer: Mike Henson
Creative Director: Malena Stojić
Associate Publisher: Holly Willsher
Production Manager: Nikki Ingram

No part of this publication may be reproduced, stored in a retrieval system,
or transmitted in any form or by any means, electronic, mechanical,
photocopying, recording, or otherwise, without the prior permission
of the publisher or a license permitting restricted copying.

All rights reserved.

ISBN: 978-1-83600-251-2

9 8 7 6 5 4 3 2 1

Manufactured in Guangdong, China TT052025

I'M NOT SCARY...

I'M JUST A DINOSAUR!

BEN LERWILL
ERICA SALCEDO

words&pictures

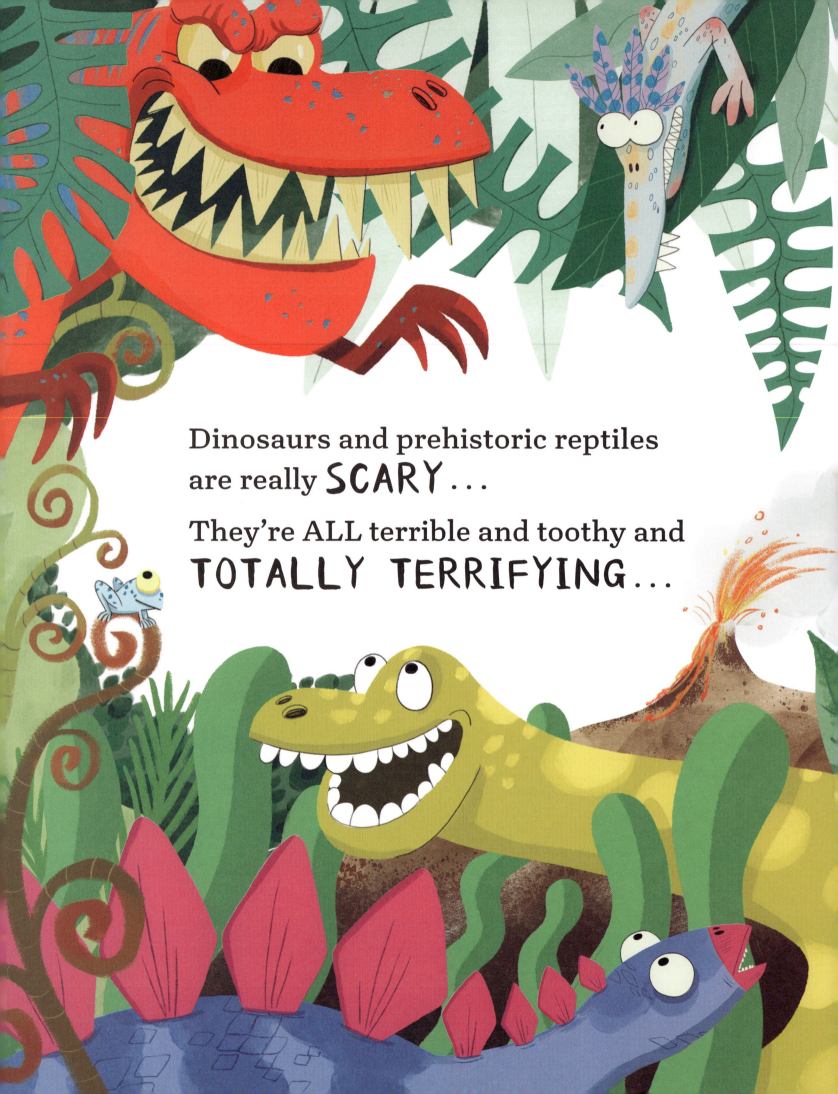

Dinosaurs and prehistoric reptiles are really SCARY...

They're ALL terrible and toothy and TOTALLY TERRIFYING...

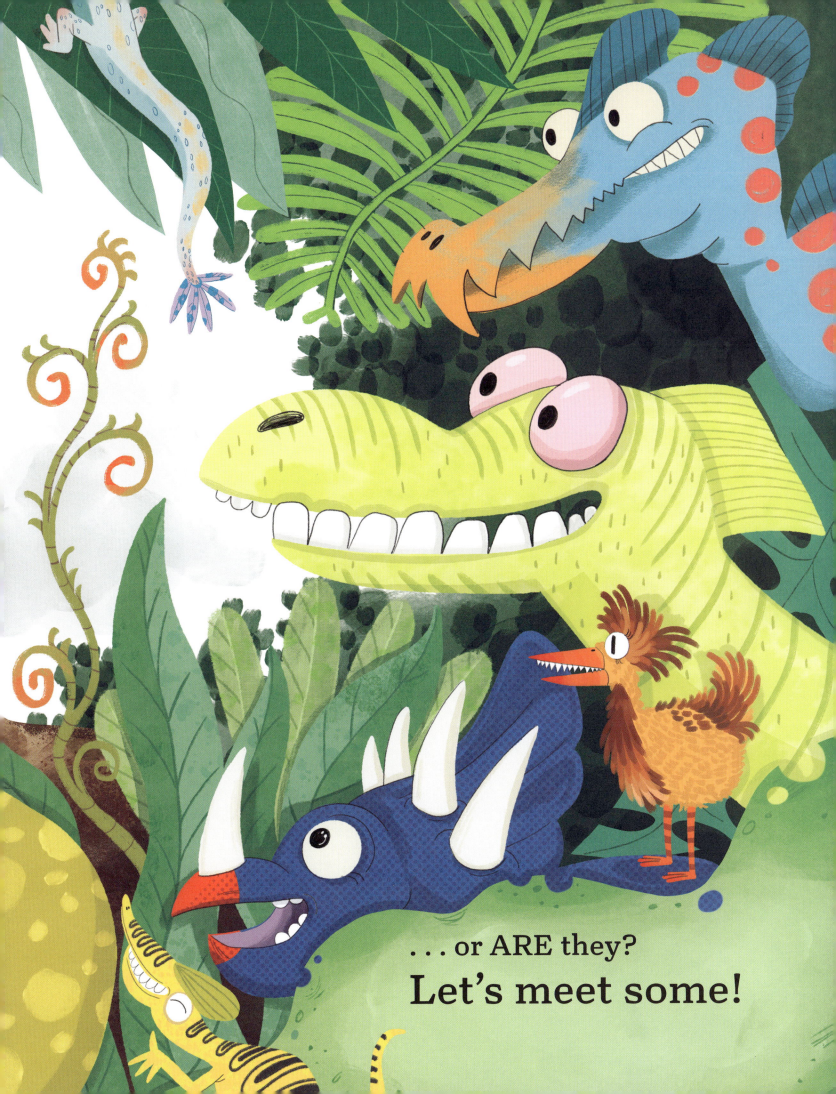

... or ARE they?
Let's meet some!

I'm a **Pteranodon**.
My huge wings are as **WIDE** as a car!

But they're nothing to worry about!
They help me glide through the sky.

I'm a **Stegosaurus**. My back is covered with big, pointy plates.

They look kind of funny, but they're very helpful. They let other Stegosauruses know who I am!

I'm a **Corythosaurus**.
My back legs are big and strong.

But I have them for a reason...
They help me stand up and
walk around on two feet.

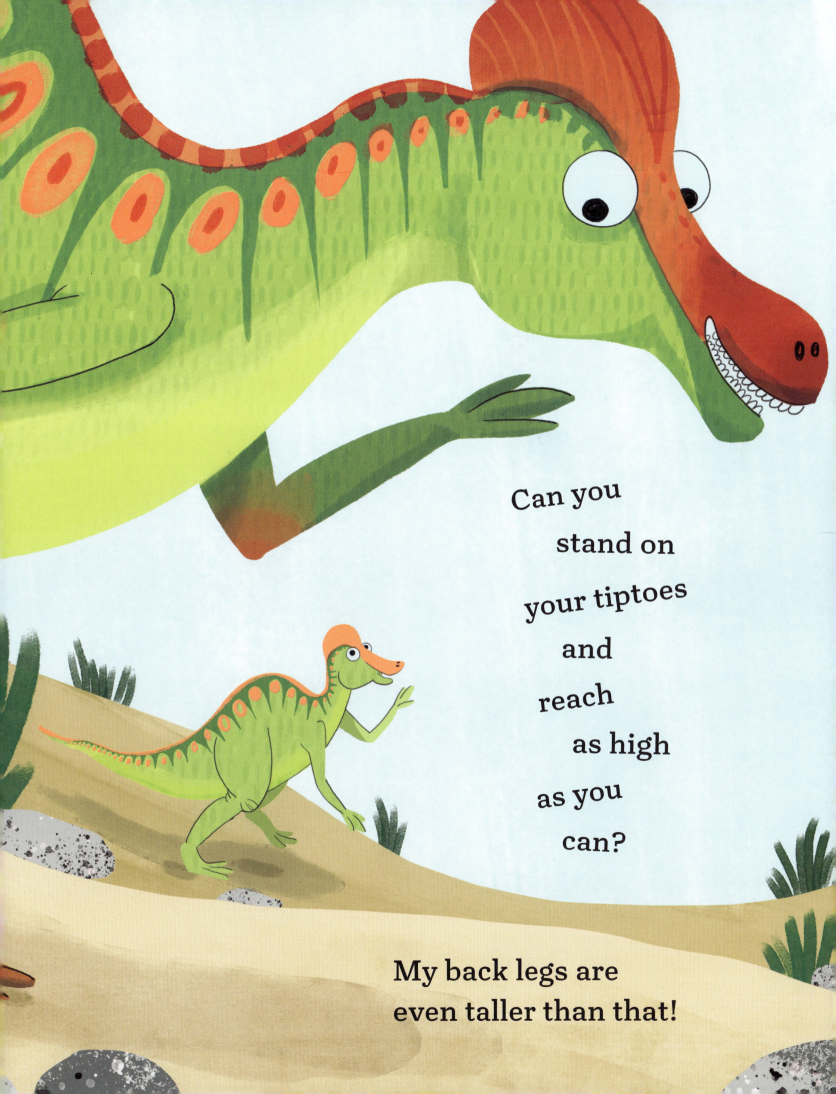

Can you stand on your tiptoes and reach as high as you can?

My back legs are even taller than that!

I'm an **Iguanodon**.
I have a strange beak and powerful teeth.

But they're not terrifying at all!
They help me chew on delicious plants.

Is there something in my teeth?

I'm an **Ankylosaurus**.
My body is covered in thick, bumpy skin.

But it's nothing to be frightened of.
It acts like a shield and keeps me
from getting hurt.

I'm a Triceratops.
The huge frill around my head is spiky.

But it's not meant to be scary!
It protects my neck and makes me look
LOVELY to other Triceratops.

Hey, good looking!

I'm a **Velociraptor**. I'm super-speedy, with sharp teeth and claws.

But don't be afraid—I'm only small! My fast legs help me race across the ground.

WHOOSH!

How fast can you run?
Ready, set... GO!

I'm a Brachiosaurus.
I have a long neck and an absolutely HUMONGOUS body!

But I'm not frightening. Being so huge makes me pretty slow. Even walking up hills is tiring for me!

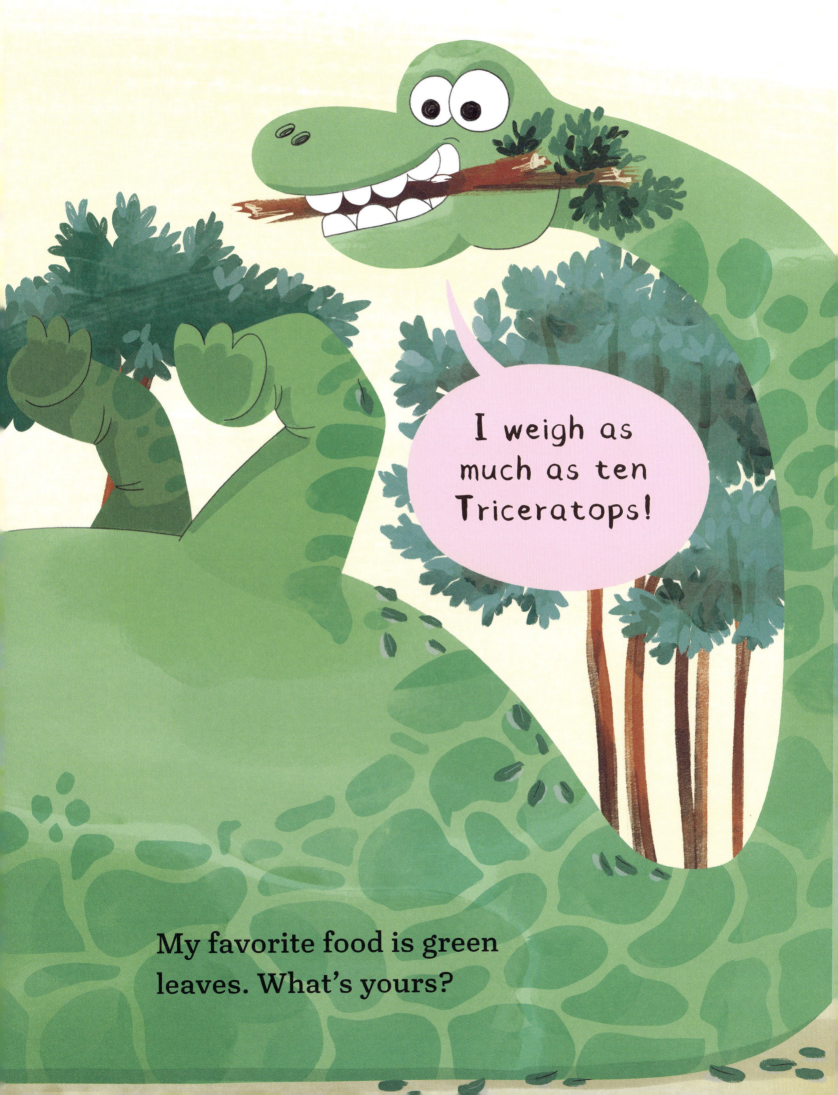

I'm an **Ichthyosaurus**.
My big, round eyes might look spooky.

But I'd be lost without them!
They help me see where I'm
going in the deep, dark water.

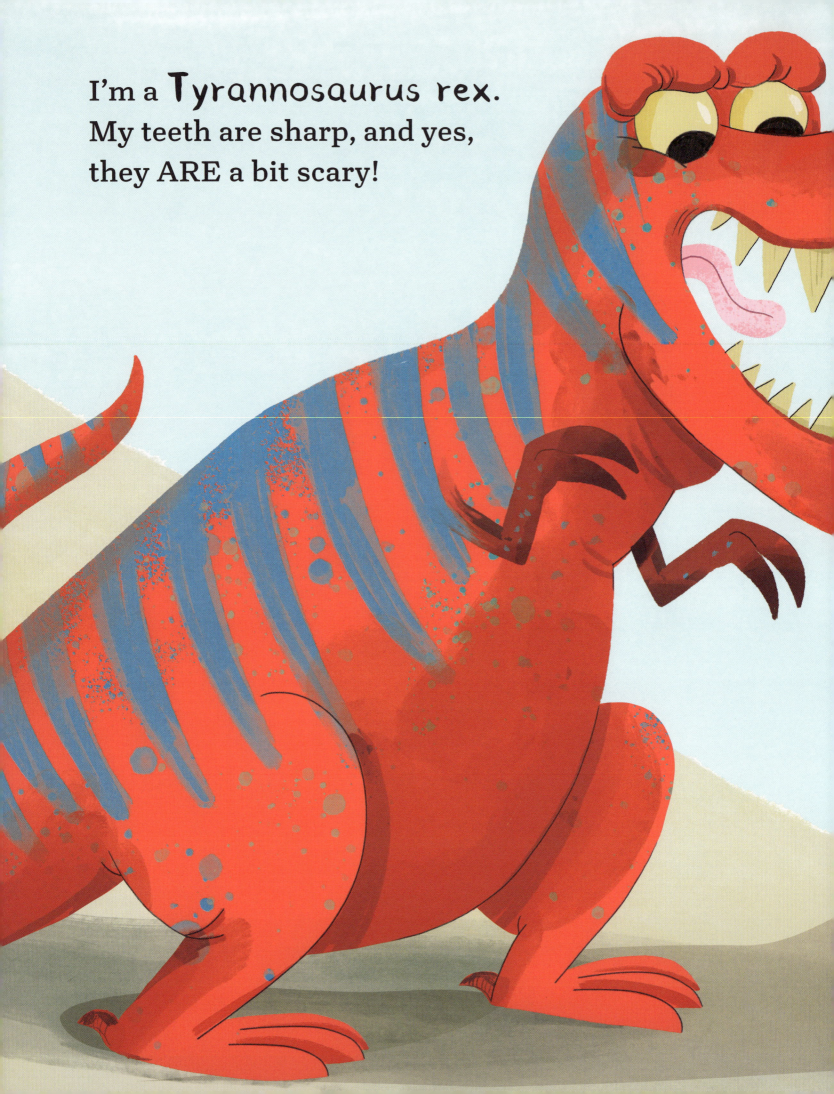

But YOU don't need to worry. They help me catch food for me and my babies to eat.

I may have big teeth, but I have tiny arms!

Can you give a great big T. rex grin and show all YOUR teeth?

Dinosaurs came in all shapes and sizes. Some were huge, some were tiny—and some looked very strange!

But have you ever wondered why?

To survive, animals need to find food, stay safe, and take care of themselves and their families. Just like today's animals, different dinosaurs had different ways of surviving.

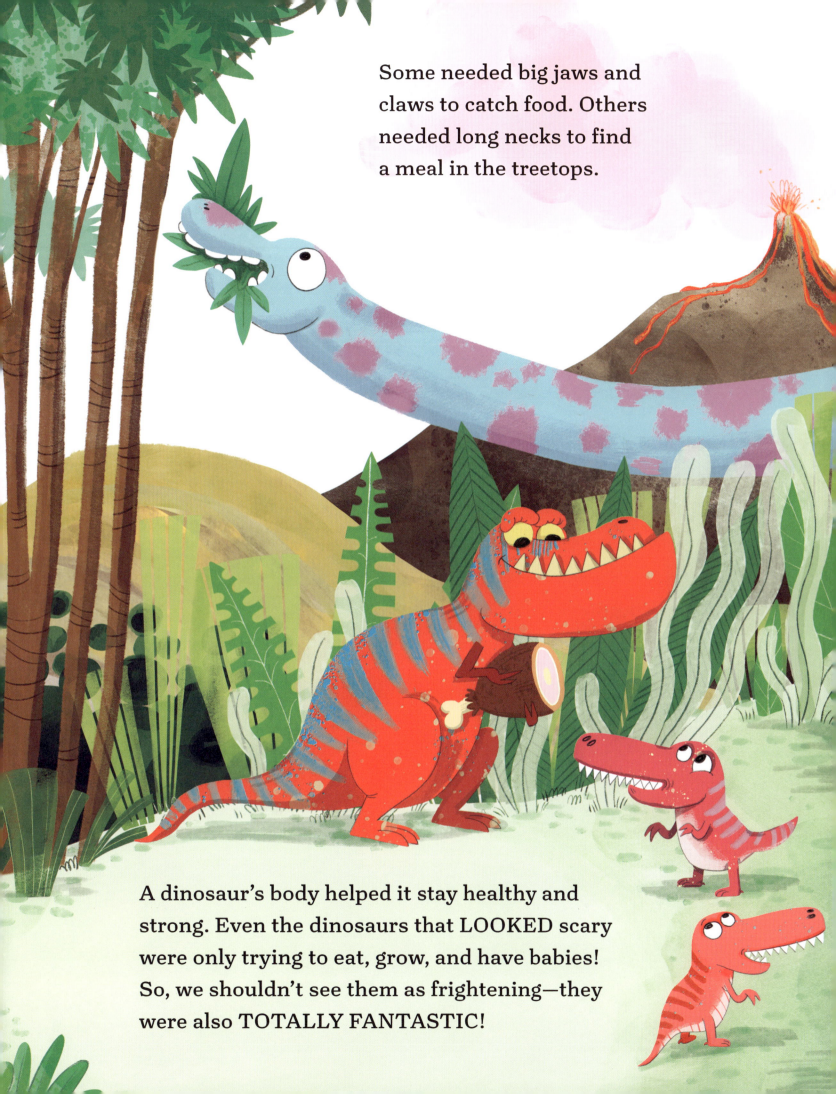

Some needed big jaws and claws to catch food. Others needed long necks to find a meal in the treetops.

A dinosaur's body helped it stay healthy and strong. Even the dinosaurs that LOOKED scary were only trying to eat, grow, and have babies! So, we shouldn't see them as frightening—they were also TOTALLY FANTASTIC!

Most dinosaurs became extinct more than 65 million years ago, but some of today's animals share their features.

Amazingly, all birds are descended from dinosaurs—even the small ones you see in your yard! Lots of them have three forward toes and one backward toe on each foot, just like a T. rex.

Dinosaurs were reptiles. A reptile is a kind of animal with a backbone and scaly skin. Lots of today's reptiles have very special bodies, too. . .

Geckos have large eyes for spotting insects to eat.

Chameleons have special feet that help them walk on branches.

Crocodiles have tough, bumpy skin to protect themselves.

Snakes have jaws that can open wide to help them catch food.

Sea turtles have hard beaks to help them chomp on sea grasses.

Ben Lerwill is an award-winning writer and author from England. He lives in Oxfordshire, UK, close to where the world's first dinosaur fossils were found, and one of his earliest memories is of staring up at Dippy the Diplodocus in London's Natural History Museum. He has two children, one dog, and no Velociraptors.

Erica Salcedo is an illustrator, born and raised in Cuenca, Spain. She graduated in Fine Arts from the University of Castilla-La Mancha, before taking a Master's degree in graphic design and illustration at the Polytechnic University of Valencia. Erica has spent the last 12 years drawing a lot of pets and drinking a lot of tea. If she were a dinosaur, she'd probably be a *Tea*-Rex.